# MERCER MAYER'S
# CRITTERS OF THE NIGHT ™

# IF YOU DREAM A DRAGON

### Written by Erica Farber and J. R. Sansevere

## A Random House PICTUREBACK®
## Random House 🏠 New York

Copyright © 1996 Big Tuna Trading Company, LLC.
CRITTERS OF THE NIGHT™ and all prominent characters featured in this book and the distinctive likenesses thereof are trademarks of Big Tuna Trading Company, LLC. All rights reserved under International and Pan-American Copyright Conventions. Published in the United States by Random House, Inc., New York, and simultaneously in Canada by Random House of Canada Limited, Toronto.
http://www.randomhouse.com/
*Library of Congress Cataloging-in-Publication Data*
Farber, Erica. If you dream a dragon / by Erica Farber & J. R. Sansevere ; illustrated by Mercer Mayer.
p. cm. — (Critters of the night) (A Random House pictureback) SUMMARY: When the Great Wazoo kidnaps all the baby dragons, Axel Howl must be the knight in shining armor who rescues them. ISBN 0-679-87374-0 (pbk) [1. Dragons—Fiction. ] I. Sansevere, John R. II. Mayer, Mercer, 1943- ill. III. Title. IV. Series: Mayer, Mercer, 1943- PZ7.F2275If 1996 [E]—dc20 96-14231
Printed in the United States of America    10 9 8 7 6 5 4 3 2 1

A BIG TUNA TRADING COMPANY, LLC/J. R. SANSEVERE BOOK

Last night I dreamt about a dragon.
And you know what?
That dragon came looking for me.
He flew right in my window.

I jumped out of bed and put on my armor and I walked right up to that dragon. Then he started to cry. He told me that the Great Wazoo had stolen all the baby dragons.

A knight in shining armor had to rescue them, pronto.
Guess who was the knight in shining armor? Me, of course!

So I hopped on the dragon's back and I said,
"To the castle of the Great Wazoo, on the double!"

The dragon and I flew out the window
and up into the sky.
We flew through the night to the big,
black castle of the Great Wazoo . . .

The door to the castle was shut tight.
There was no way in and no way out.
But I knew just what to do.
"Fly around the castle nine times," I told the dragon.
All knights know that nine is the magic number.

So the dragon and I flew around the castle
once . . . twice . . . three times . . .
  when out of the darkness came nine big, black birds.
    They gnashed their beaks and they snapped
      their claws and they tried to catch us.
        Four more times around we flew . . .
          five . . . six . . . seven . . . eight . . .

Just as those black birds were about to get us, we flew around the castle for the ninth time. Then you know what happened? The castle door opened, and we flew right in!

The castle door slammed shut behind us.
And those nine black birds fell
splash-splunk into the moat,
which was filled with bubbly green goo.

The dragon and I tiptoed through
a secret passageway until we got
to the Great Hall.

There, on a big throne, sat the Great Wazoo himself.
He was counting his gold and eating chocolate cake.

I pulled out my sword and I charged right up
to the Great Wazoo.
"Let those baby dragons go!" I yelled.
"Never!" shouted the Great Wazoo.
Then the Great Wazoo blew
his big gold whistle.
And guess who flew
into the Great Hall?

Those nine black birds.
They were covered with green goo.
And, boy, were they mad!
They gnashed their beaks and they snapped their claws
and they headed right for the dragon and me . . .

So I jumped on top of the Great Wazoo and tickled him as hard as I could. The Great Wazoo burst out laughing. And then you know what happened?

The evil spell of the Great Wazoo was broken!
Those black birds began to sing.
Then they flew into the kitchen and baked a pie.
Guess who they put in the pie?

The Great Wazoo himself!
The black birds invited the dragon and me for pie and milk.
But we had to go. We had a job to do.

The dragon and I ran down to the dungeon lickety-split,
and we set all the baby dragons free.
Boy, were those baby dragons happy to see us!
They kissed us and hugged us until I said, "Home, dragon!"

So the dragon and I flew home, with all the baby dragons flying right behind us.

So if you ever dream about a dragon, don't be scared.
He's just looking for a knight in shining armor!
He's just looking for *you!*